Jingle Spells

James Brown

SIMON & SCHUSTER

London New York Sydney Toronto New Delhi

Now, if there's one thing every witch LOVES, it's Halloween.

They love gobbling gloop-filled gobstoppers . . .

Trixie's potion

. . . and playing party tricks and games.

love your library

Buckinghamshire Libraries

Search, renew or reserve online 24/7
www.buckscc.gov.uk/libraries

24 hour renewal line
0303 123 0035

Enquiries
01296 382415

Santa

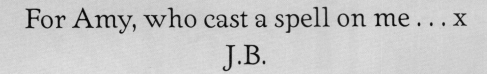

For Amy, who cast a spell on me . . . x
J.B.

SIMON & SCHUSTER
First published in Great Britain in 2018 by Simon & Schuster UK Ltd
1st Floor, 222 Gray's Inn Road, London, WC1X 8HB • A CBS Company
Text and illustrations copyright © 2018 James Brown • The right of James Brown to be
identified as the author and illustrator of this work has been asserted by him in accordance
with the Copyright, Designs and Patents Act, 1988 • All rights reserved, including the right
of reproduction in whole or in part in any form • A CIP catalogue record for this book is
available from the British Library upon request.
978-1-4711-7058-4 (PB) • 978-1-4711-7060-7 (eBook)
Printed in China • 10 9 8 7 6 5 4 3 2 1

But this little witch was different.
Trixie loved . . .

...CHRISTMAS!

"Jingle spells, jingle spells,
Jingle all the way!
Oh, what fun it is to wish
For the joy of Christmas Day!"

She looked forward to it more than anything.

Her friends thought she was as batty as a vampire.

"If ONLY I could make them understand how magical Christmas is," Trixie sighed.

Then she had an idea.
"I know! I'll write to Santa for help!"

But when the reply arrived, it wasn't the news she'd been hoping for.

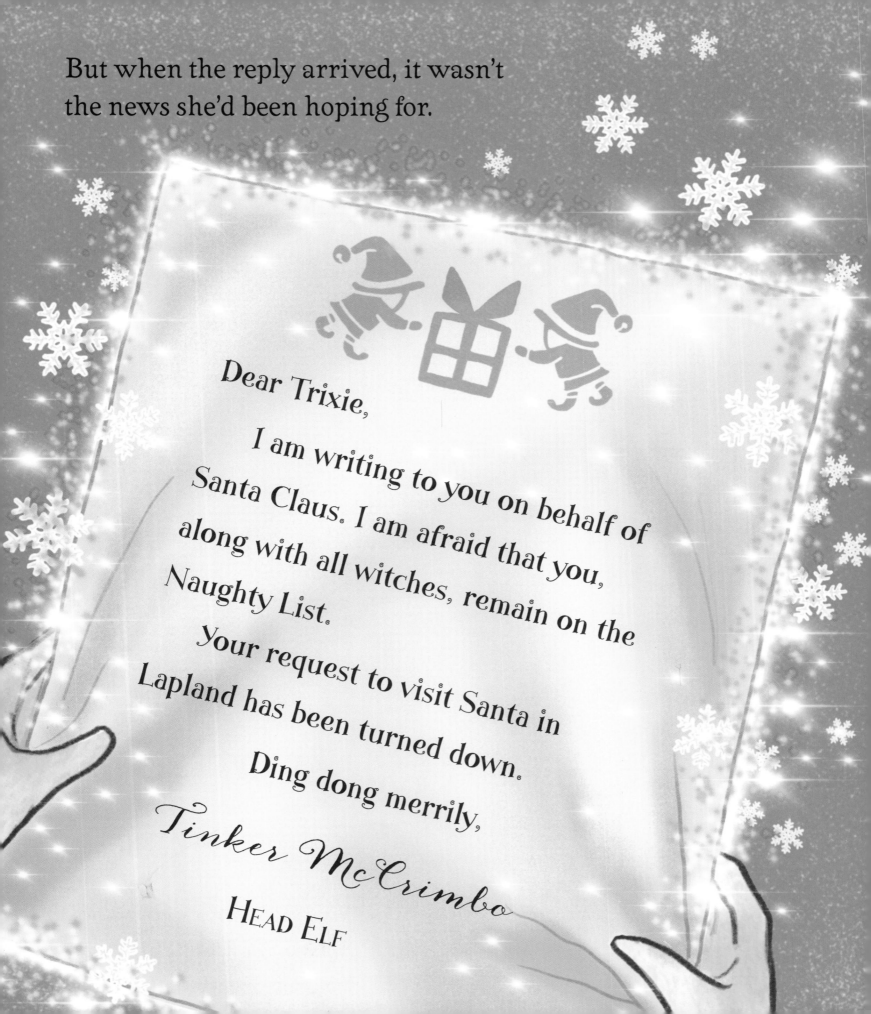

Dear Trixie,

I am writing to you on behalf of Santa Claus. I am afraid that you, along with all witches, remain on the Naughty List.

Your request to visit Santa in Lapland has been turned down.

Ding dong merrily,

Tinker McCrimbo

HEAD ELF

"Naughty List?" Trixie said to Rudy the cat.
"I'm not naughty! If I could just see Santa,
I know he'd help me.

Come on, let's go!"

And with a WHOOSH
they were off!

Through the snowy skies they flew,
whirling and twirling
like snowflakes in the wind until . . .

. . . BUMPETY

BUMP,

they landed THUMP! Right in front
of Santa's workshop.

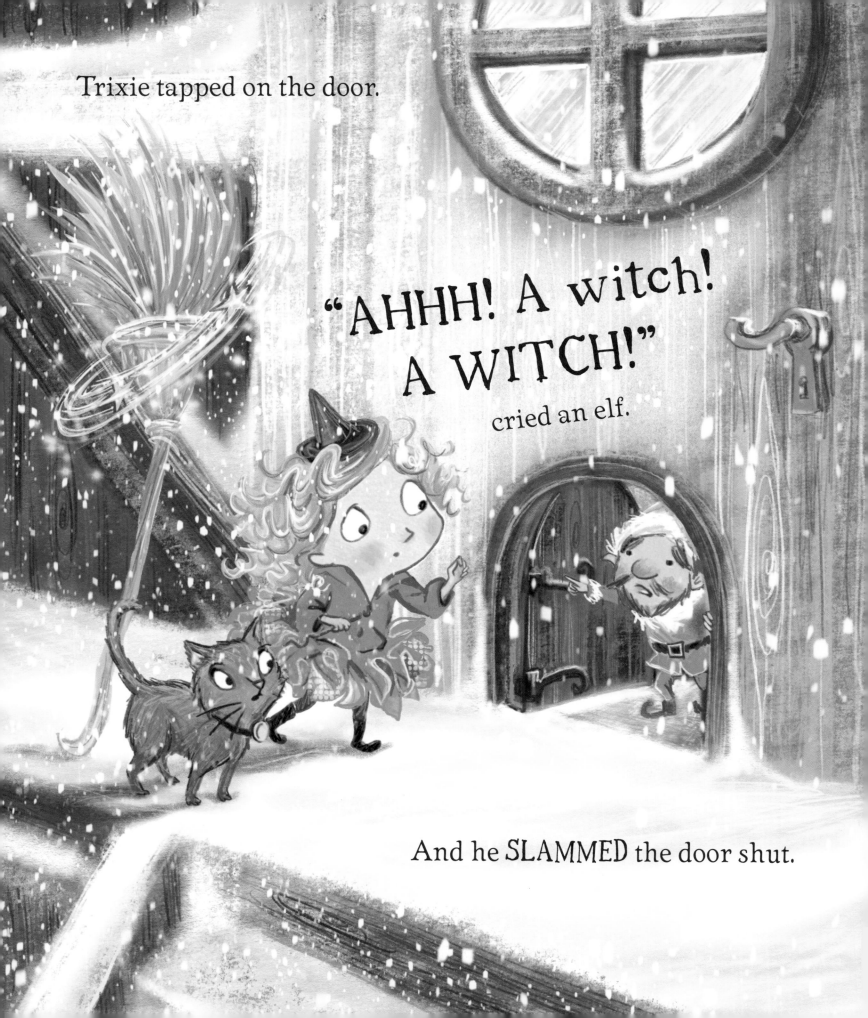

Trixie tapped on the door.

"AHHH! A witch! A WITCH! A WITCH!"
cried an elf.

And he SLAMMED the door shut.

"How odd," frowned Trixie.
"But we've come too far to give up now."
And with a clickety-click of her fingers . . .

DING! They were in the workshop.
But it wasn't what she'd imagined . . .

The elves' shelves were almost empty!
Where was Santa? WHAT was going on?

Then Trixie heard a loud,

"AAAACHOO!"

"They've all got colds!" she gasped.
"I've got to help or the toys will never
be ready in time for Christmas!"

First, Trixie tried a STICK TOGETHER spell.
But that didn't work.

So she cast a WRAP UP WELL spell.
But that only made things worse!

"What's going on?"
one elf spluttered.

"That naughty witch is playing tr-tr-tricks!" sneezed another.

But Trixie wasn't being tricksy. Everything was in a muddle and she didn't know WHAT to do.

She thought hard.

"When my friends are poorly, it's not my SPELLS that make them feel warm inside . . .

. . . it's my special potion!"
And with a sweep of her wand
a cauldron appeared.

"Jingle spells, jingle spells,
Jingle colds away!

Oh, how nice it is to sip
From a nice warm mug today!"

"I'm not drinking THAT,"
grumbled an elf.

"It looks like your
snot," said another.

Suddenly, Trixie heard a "HO HO HO-CHOO!"
Could it possibly be . . . ?

Yes! It was Santa!

But he was as wheezy and weary as everyone else.

"Ah, a nice hot drink. How kind!"
And Santa took one, long gulp.

The elves gasped.

Would he turn into a candy frog?
Or a pumpkin pudding?

"It's as sweet as Christmas!" beamed Santa.
"Who made this?"

"It was me, Trixie."

"Well I never," Santa said, "what a nice witch you are."

One by one, the elves took a cautious sip,
warmth soaring through them.

And, as if by magic . . .

. . . they were back to work, stitching, sticking and singing away:

"Jingle spells, jingle spells,
Jingle all the way!
Oh, what fun it is to make
New toys for Christmas Day!"

"Now," Santa said, "what's your Christmas wish, Trixie?"
"I just want to share it with my friends," she sighed,
"but I can't make them understand how magical it is."

"Ho ho ho! You share Christmas
joy every day," chuckled Santa,
"but I can give you a bit of help . . ."

So, that special night, with a
sprinkle of Santa's magic,
Trixie brought Christmas . . .

. . . to everyone!

Because this little witch knows
how to trick AND treat!